Hurry Granny Annie

Arlene Alda
Illustrations by Eve Aldridge

TRICYCLE PRESS
Berkeley · Toronto

TRICYCLE PRESS
a little division of Ten Speed Press
P.O. Box 7123
Berkeley, California 94707
www.tenspeed.com

Book design by Susan Van Horn
Typeset in Contemporary Brush

Library of Congress Cataloging-in-Publication Data
Alda, Arlene, 1933–
    Hurry Granny Annie / Arlene Alda; illustrations by Eve Aldridge.
        p.   cm.
    Summary: One after another three children chase after Granny Annie
who is running to "catch" something great.
    ISBN-13: 978-1-883672-72-0 hc / ISBN-13: 978-1-58246-067-3 pbk
    ISBN-10: 1-883672-72-4 hc / ISBN-10: 1-58246-067-1 pbk
    [1. Sun—Rising and setting—Fiction.]   I. Aldridge, Eve, ill.   II. Title.
PZ7.A34Hu   1999   99–11180
                                                                          CIP

First printing, 1999
First paperback printing, 2002

Printed in China

2 3 4 5 6 — 09 08 07 06 05

For Olivia, Jake, Isabel,
Scott, and Emilia.
— A. A.

For Aida and the Sunday run.
With a special heartfelt thanks to
Armin, Tirzah, and Talya.
— E. A.

It was a sunny autumn day. Granny Annie ran by the fishing hole so fast, it looked just like a train had passed.

Little Ruthie looked up from fishing and shouted to Granny Annie, "Why are you running so fast? Is it going to rain?"

"Have to hurry. Can't be late.
Catching something. Something great,"
said Granny Annie, whizzing by.

"Wait for me. I'm a fast runner," said Ruthie.
"And I'd sure like to catch something great," she
added, with her fishing pole in hand.

So off they went, up a hill, down a path, through a grove of trees.

And *just* as Granny Annie
was about to tell Ruthie what
she was going to catch—

the dust in the road made her sneeze.

"AchooOOo!"

They passed Ruthie's brother Joe
in the baseball field.

"What's happening? Are you running
to a fire?" he asked.

"Have to hurry. Can't be late.
Catching something. Something great,"
said Granny Annie.

"I know how to hurry," said Joe. "But what are you catching?" he asked, running with his mitt.

"Come on," said Ruthie to Joe. "We'll find out later."

So off they went, over some grass, onto a field, awfully close to some bees.

And *just* as Granny Annie
was about to tell Joe what she
was going to catch—

some pollen made her sneeze.

"AchooOoo!"

They soon passed Charlie's house. Charlie was in his yard with his new butterfly net.

"Is something chasing you guys?" Charlie asked. "Is it a skunk?"

"Have to hurry. Can't be late.
Catching something. Something
great," said Granny Annie, with Ruthie
and Joe in a line behind her.

"Can I come too?" asked Charlie. "I promise to
help you catch whatever it is," he said, swinging
his butterfly net over his shoulder.

"Come on," said Ruthie, Joe, and Granny Annie.

So off they went across a bridge, into a marsh, almost up to their knees.

And *just* as Granny Annie was about to tell Charlie what she was going to catch—

the dampness made her sneeze.

Then they reached the end of the road where the ocean began.

"We got here just in time!" said Granny Annie. "We came to catch something great and we did! We got here in time to catch the sunset!"

Ruthie, Joe, and Charlie said together in one loud voice, "CATCH THE SUNSET?!"

Granny Annie thought for a minute. "If I hadn't sneezed," she said, "I would have told you that's why I was running."

Joe said, "I thought you meant catch a baseball with my mitt."

Charlie said, "I wanted to catch a monarch butterfly with my net."

The sun disappeared and the
sky turned from blue to pink to orange.

When the sky turned a deep purple, the sunset was over. A bright, full white moon rose in the darkening sky.

All of a sudden Granny Annie said, "Come on," and she started running towards home, fast as a train.

"Now why are you running?" asked
Ruthie, Joe, and Charlie, catching up to her.
"Have to hurry. Can't be late. This time
dinner's on your plate," said Granny Annie.
So off went Ruthie, Joe, and Charlie, with
their stomachs starting to growl.

They followed Granny Annie all in a line into a marsh, across a bridge, onto a field, over some grass, up a path, down a hill, lit by the bright moonlight.

Gesundheit

It really was great. They hadn't been late. They all caught the sunset that night.